Contents

I Can Read!

BEGINNING READING 1

Ms. Turtle the Babysitter

This Book Belongs To

The Tracewell Family

by Valeri Gorbachev

HarperCollins Publishers

To Kristin Daly, Anne Hoppe, and
Stephanie Bart-Horvath

HarperCollins®, 🔲®, and I Can Read Book® are trademarks of HarperCollins Publishers Inc.

Library of Congress Cataloging-in-Publication Data
Gorbachev, Valeri.
    Ms. Turtle the babysitter / by Valeri Gorbachev. — 1st ed.
       p.   cm. — (An I can read book)
    Summary: Ms. Turtle babysits for three little frogs when their parents go out for the evening.
    ISBN-10: 0-06-058073-9 (trade bdg.) — ISBN-13: 978-0-06-058073-5 (trade bdg.)
    ISBN-10: 0-06-058074-7 (lib. bdg.) — ISBN-13: 978-0-06-058074-2 (lib. bdg.)
    ISBN-10: 0-06-058075-5 (pbk. bdg.) — ISBN-13: 978-0-06-058075-9 (pbk. bdg.)
    [1. Babysitters—Fiction.   2. Frogs—Fiction.   3. Turtles—Fiction.]   I. Title.   II. Series.
PZ7.G6475Ms   2005   2004006234
[E]—dc22   CIP
                                                                                                          AC

❖

Ms. Turtle's Promise

Mother and Father Frog
were going to a party.
Ms. Turtle came to babysit.

"Hello, Little Frogs,"
said Ms. Turtle.
"What are we going to do tonight?
Would you like me
to read you a story?"
"Yes, yes!" said the little frogs.
"We would like that very much!"

Ms. Turtle finished reading.

The little frogs cried,

"Would you like to jump

with us now, Ms. Turtle?"

"Not now," said Ms. Turtle.

"It's supper time.

I will make you a nice supper."

"Okay," said the little frogs.

"We are very hungry."

The little frogs ate their supper.
"That was yummy," they said.
"Will you jump with us now?"
"Not now," said Ms. Turtle.

"Now it is time for music," she said.

"I will sing a song with you."

"Okay," said the little frogs.

"We love to sing!"

And they sang, "Croak, Croak, Croak,"

as loud as they could.

When they finished singing,
the little frogs said,
"That was fun!
But we would like you
to jump with us now, Ms. Turtle!"

"Not now," said Ms. Turtle.

"Now it is bedtime.

Are you ready for bed, Little Frogs?"

13

"No!" cried the little frogs.

"We do not want to go to bed yet.

We want to jump with you,

Ms. Turtle!

Why don't you want

to jump with us?"

Ms. Turtle looked down

at the pillows.

"The truth is, I cannot jump at all,"
said Ms. Turtle. "I am sorry."

"It's too bad that you can't jump,
Ms. Turtle," said the little frogs.
"It is so much fun!"

"Yes, it is a pity," said Ms. Turtle.

"But I promise that I will learn."

"Will you jump with us
next time you come to our house?"
asked the little frogs.

"Yes, I will try," said Ms. Turtle.

"Give a promise, keep a promise.

Good night, children."

Mother and Father Frog came home.

"Ms. Turtle," they said,

"you are such a good babysitter.

Thank you for your help!"

"You are welcome," Ms. Turtle said.

She left the Frogs' house.

"What are you doing, Ms. Turtle?"
asked the neighbors.

"I am keeping a promise,"
said Ms. Turtle.
"I am learning how to jump."

Ms. Turtle's Smile

Mother and Father Frog

were going out again.

"Thank you for coming, Ms. Turtle,"

said Mother Frog.

"We're sorry to tell you
our little frogs are sad right now,
Ms. Turtle," said Father Frog.
"They don't want us to go out."

"Don't worry,
I will try to make them happy,"
said Ms. Turtle.

Mother and Father Frog left.

Ms. Turtle asked the little frogs,

"Do you want to play a game?"

"No," said the little frogs.

"We don't want to."

"Would you like to dance?"
asked Ms. Turtle.
"No," said the little frogs.
"We don't want to."

"I learned how to jump,"
said Ms. Turtle.

"Let's jump rope!"

"No," said the little frogs.

"We don't want to."

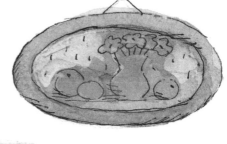

The little frogs looked
sadder than ever.
"When you little frogs are sad,
I am sad too," Ms. Turtle said.
She sat down. She was very sad.
The little frogs looked
at Ms. Turtle.

"It is our fault

that Ms. Turtle is so sad," they said.

"We should make her happy again."

"Let's play a drum for her,"
said the first little frog.
"Maybe that will make her happy."
"We could draw a picture for her,"
said the second little frog.
"Maybe that will make her happy."
"No, I have a better idea,"
said the third little frog.
"To make her happy,
first we must make her smile.
And I know how!"

"Let's get dressed up and
make ourselves look funny!"
said the third little frog.

"That is a great idea,"
said the other little frogs.
They all snuck away and
put on funny clothes.

"Ms. Turtle!"

the little frogs cried.

"Look at us!"

"Oh, there you are, Little Frogs!"

said Ms. Turtle.

"You look so funny!"

"Hooray! You are smiling,

Ms. Turtle!" cried the little frogs.

"Yes, I am," said Ms. Turtle.

And everyone was happy again.

Soon Mother and Father Frog
came home.
"Mommy! Daddy!"
cried the little frogs.
"We had so much fun!"
"I see our little frogs
do not look sad anymore,"
said Father Frog.

"How did you do it, Ms. Turtle?"
asked Mother Frog.

"It was easy," said Ms. Turtle.

"I just smiled."

Ms. Turtle's Secret

Ms. Turtle was babysitting again.

The little frogs said,

"Ms. Turtle, would you like to know

what we did on Sunday?"

"Please tell me," said Ms. Turtle.

"We went to the circus," they said.

"And would you like to know
a secret, Ms. Turtle?" they asked.
"Yes," said Ms. Turtle.
"I would love to."
"We love the circus.
We want to be in the circus,"
said the little frogs.

"I want to be a tiger tamer,"
said the first little frog.
"The bravest tiger tamer
in the circus. That is my secret."

"And I want to be a strong man,"
said the second little frog.
"The strongest in the circus.
That is my secret."

"And I want to be a juggler,"
said the third little frog.
"The best juggler in the circus.
That is my secret."

"Thank you for sharing your secrets with me," said Ms. Turtle.

"Would you like to know my secret?"

"Yes, yes!" cried the little frogs.

"Do you want to be in the circus too, Ms. Turtle?"

"You could be a trapeze artist,"
said the first little frog.

"Or you could be a bareback rider,"
said the second little frog.

"Or you could be a clown,"
said the third little frog.

"No, no, no," said Ms. Turtle.
"I don't want to be in the circus.
But I want to watch you perform,
and I want to clap louder
than anyone else. That is my secret."

"We love your secret, Ms. Turtle,"
said the little frogs.

"And I love you, Little Frogs,"
said Ms. Turtle.